ARE THE DINOSAURS DEAD, DAD?

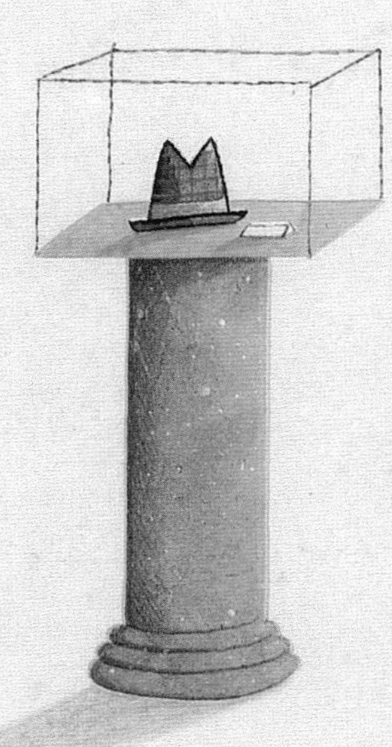

Julie Middleton

illustrated by Russell Ayto

PEACHTREE
ATLANTA

For Sam, Frankie, and Harley J.M.

For Alyx, Greta, Emilio, and Loveday—
I'm not extinct, just busy! R.A.

Thanks to Kerry Cornwell, Geology Program Manager at the Tellus Science Museum in Cartersville, Georgia, for her assistance in verifying the dinosaur facts among the dinosaur fiction.

Published by
PEACHTREE PUBLISHERS
1700 Chattahoochee Avenue
Atlanta, Georgia 30318-2112
www.peachtree-online.com

First published in Great Britain in 2012 by Picture Corgi, an imprint of Random House Children's Books
First United States version published in 2013 by Peachtree Publishers.

The illustrations were rendered in pen and ink, watercolor, pencil crayon, and collage.

Printed in May 2013 by Toppan Leefung in China
10 9 8 7 6 5 4 3 2

Library of Congress Cataloging-in-Publication Data

Middleton, Julie, 1960-
Are the dinosaurs dead, Dad? / written by Julie Middleton ; illustrated by Russell Ayto.
pages cm
Summary: Touring the museum's dinosaur exhibit, Dave's father remains oblivious
as the prehistoric animals spring to life.
ISBN 978-1-56145-690-1 / 1-56145-690-X
[1. Dinosaurs--Fiction. 2. Father and child--Fiction.] I. Ayto, Russell, illustrator. II. Title.
PZ7.M587Ar 2013
[E]--dc23
2012025716

"Are the dinosaurs dead, Dad?"
asked Dave.

"Dead?" Dad said. "Yes, the dinosaurs are dead."

"Oh!" said Dave.

Number of Dinosaurs
Years Ago (in millions)
0

"Now, Dave," explained Dad, "this handsome fella is the **Ankylosaurus**. Look at the fabulous armor plating and bony eyelids."

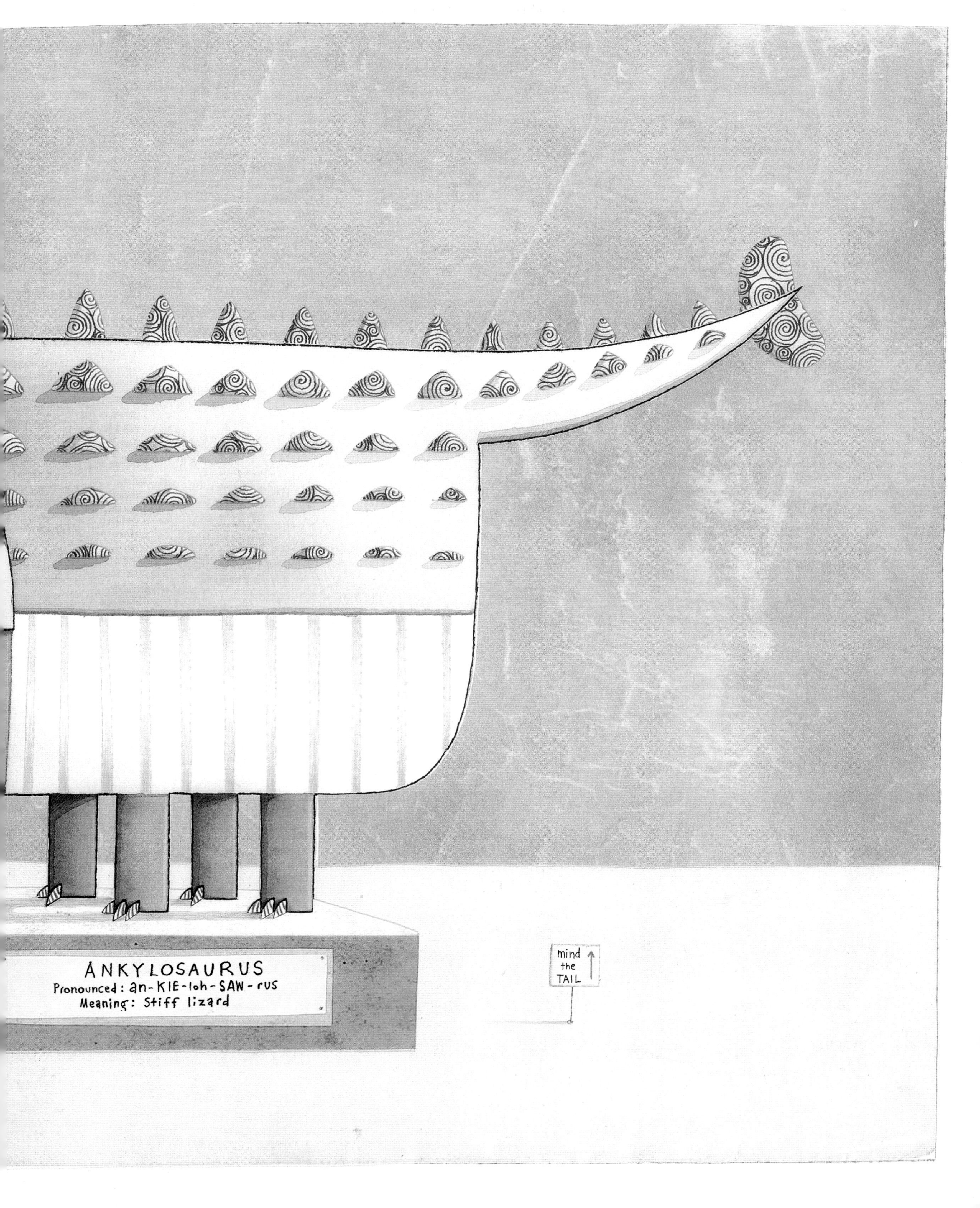
ANKYLOSAURUS
Pronounced: an-KIE-loh-SAW-rus
Meaning: Stiff lizard
mind the TAIL

"Oh," said Dave.
"It's winking at me, Dad!"

"Ankylosaurus
don't wink, Dave,"
said Dad.
"It's just your
imagination."

"You see, Dave," said Dad knowledgeably, "that dinosaur there is the **Deinocheirus**. It has some of the longest arms of all the dinosaurs."

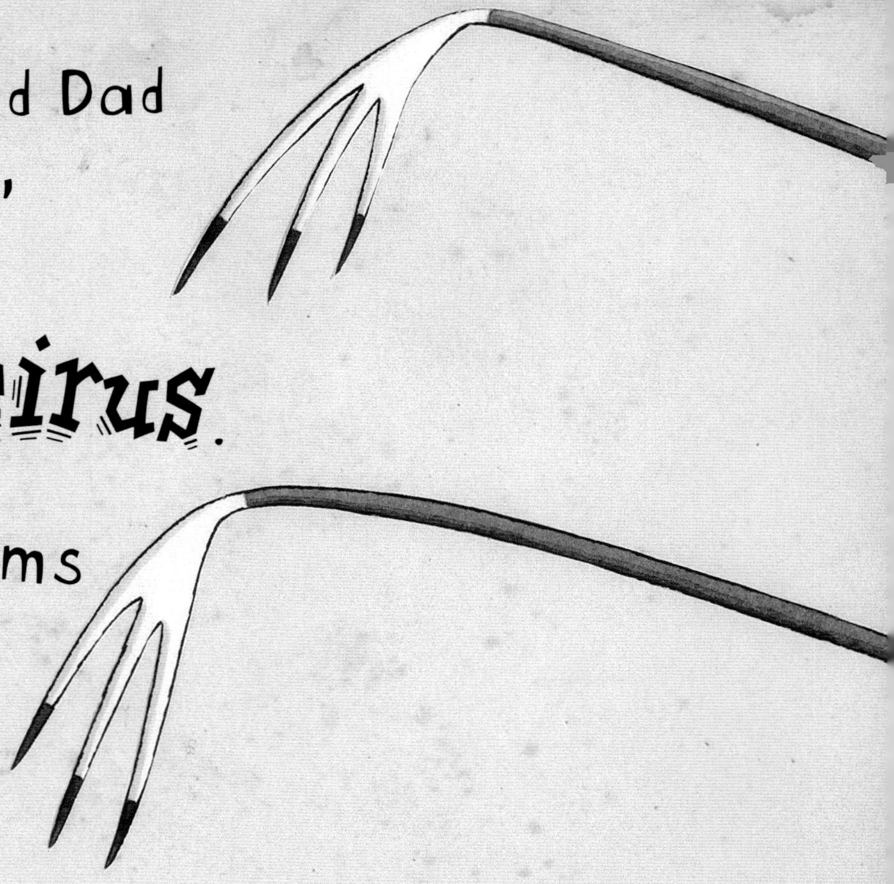

mind the hands

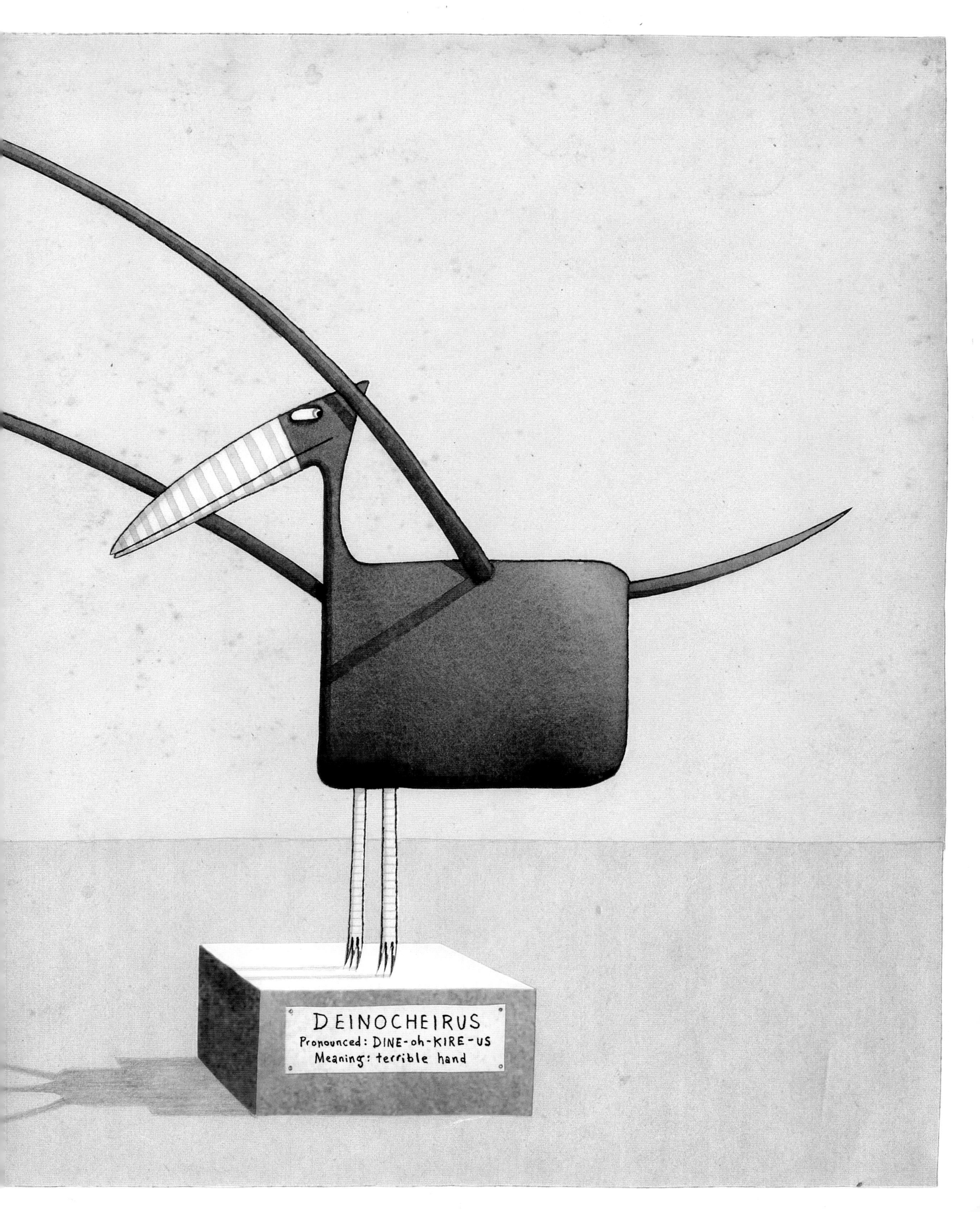
DEINOCHEIRUS
Pronounced: DINE-oh-KIRE-US
Meaning: terrible hand

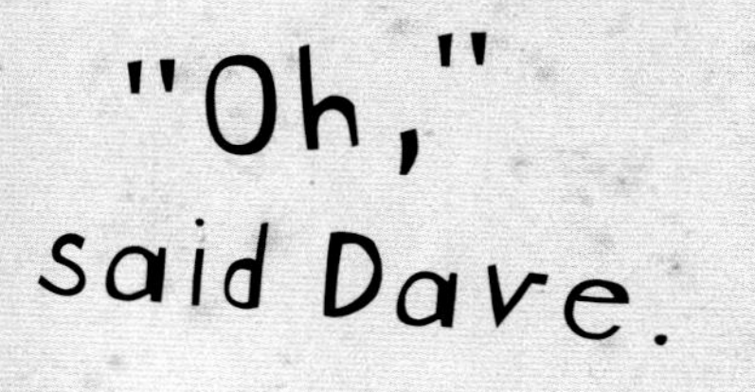

"Oh,"
said Dave.

"Why is it
trying to

tickle me, Dad?"

don't tickle, Dave,"
Dad laughed.
"It's just your
imagination."

"Now," continued Dad, "this dinosaur is the **Allosaurus**. It has long, sharp teeth."

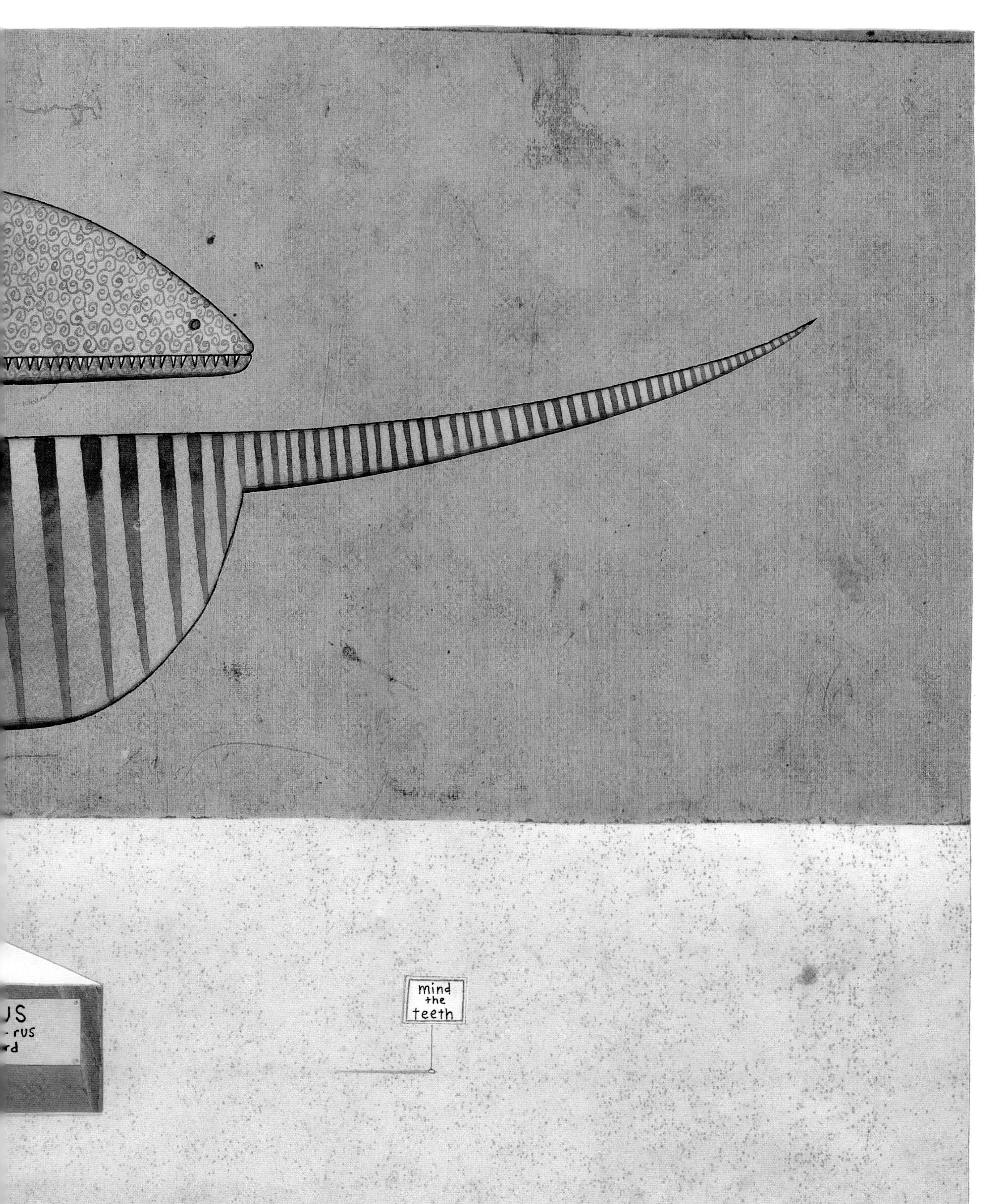
US
- rus
rd
mind the teeth

"Oh," said Dave.
"Why is it grinning
at me, Dad?"

"Allosaurus
don't grin, Dave."
Dad smiled.
"It's just your
imagination."

Dad moved on to the next dinosaur.
"Ah! You see this one with the very long neck, Dave?
DIPLODOCUS
Pronounced: dip-LOW-doh-cuss
Meaning: double beam
mind the neck

That's a Diplodocus."

"Oh," said Dave. "Why is it. . .

...trying to eat my burger?"

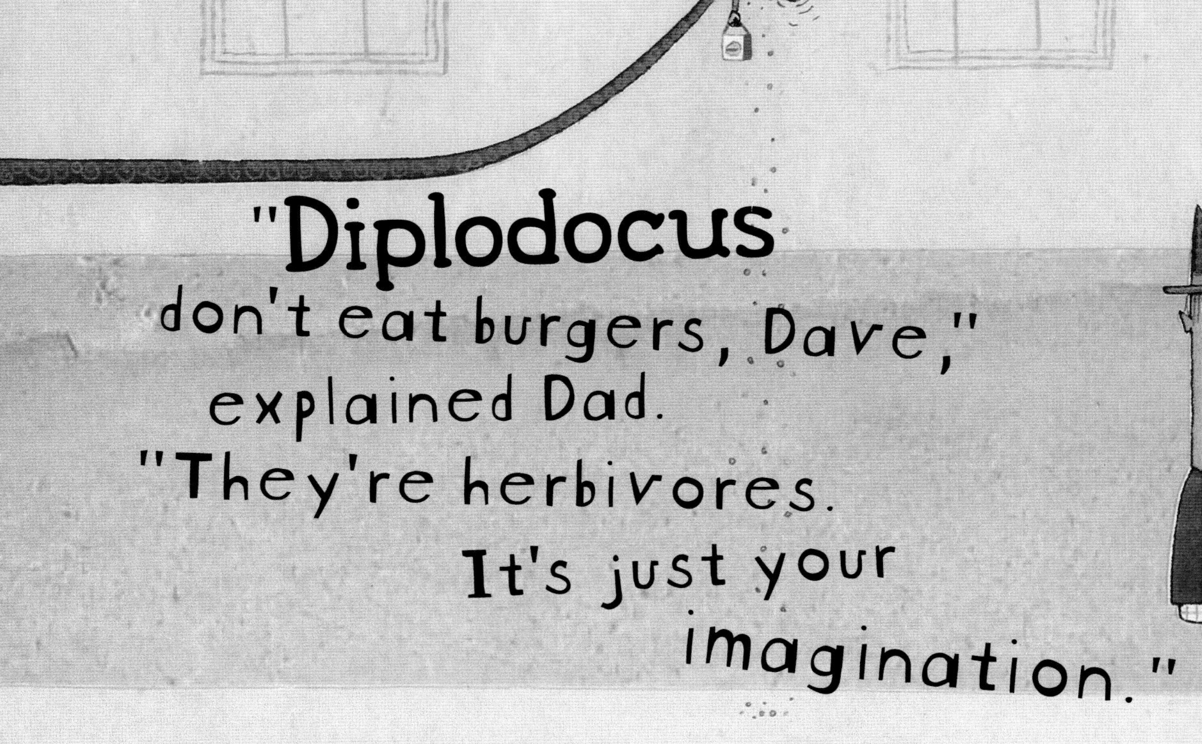

"Diplodocus
don't eat burgers, Dave,"
explained Dad.
"They're herbivores.
It's just your
imagination."

"And finally, son,
here we have the
Tyrannosaurus Rex,
one of the largest
meat-eating
dinosaurs
that
ever
lived,"
said Dad.

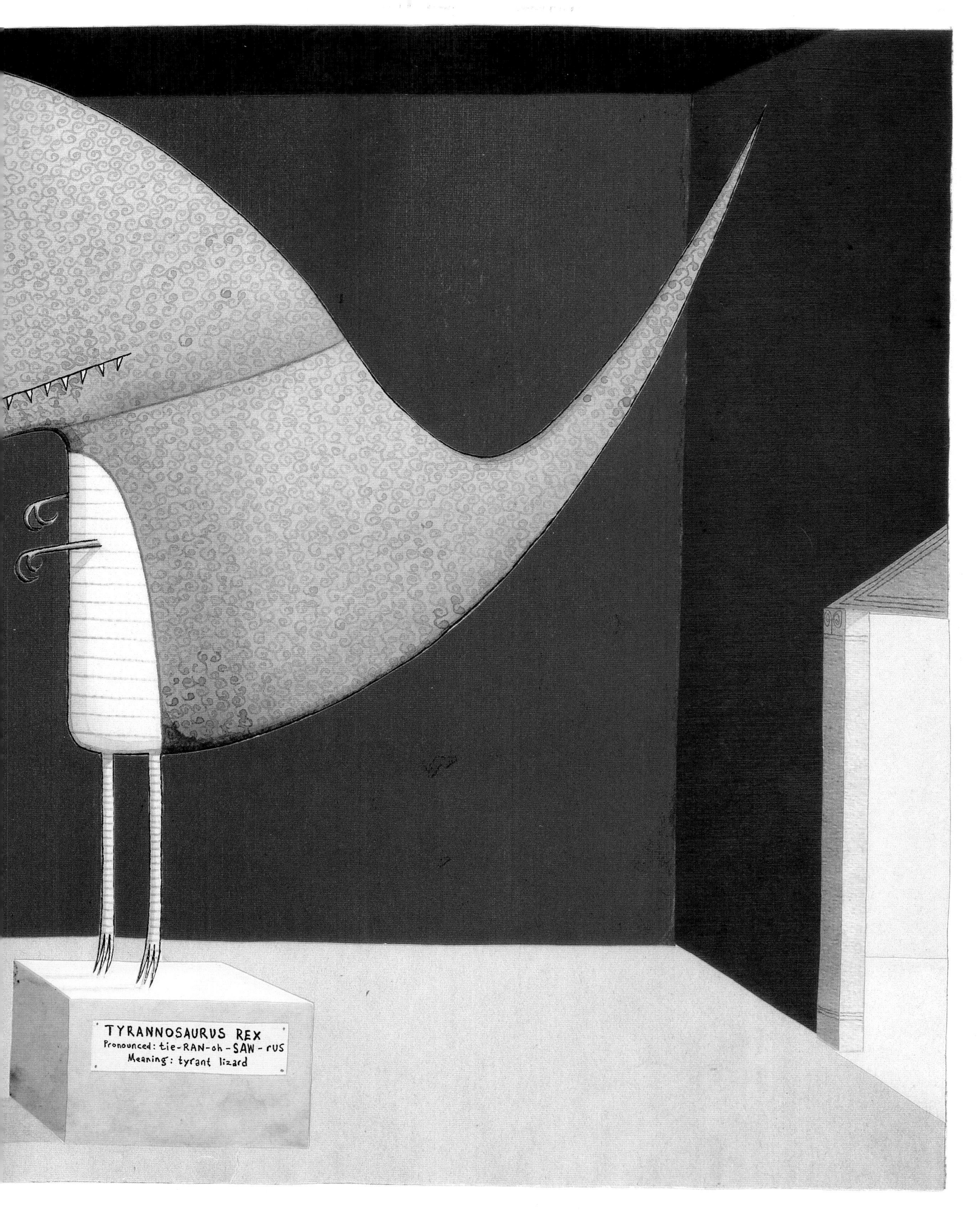
TYRANNOSAURUS REX
Pronounced: tie-RAN-oh-SAW-rus
Meaning: tyrant lizard

In Case Of Emergency
BREAK GLASS
"OH!!"
said Dave.

"So you see, Dave," said Dad, "the dinosaurs are indeed dead."

"Then why is that one

following us, Dad?"

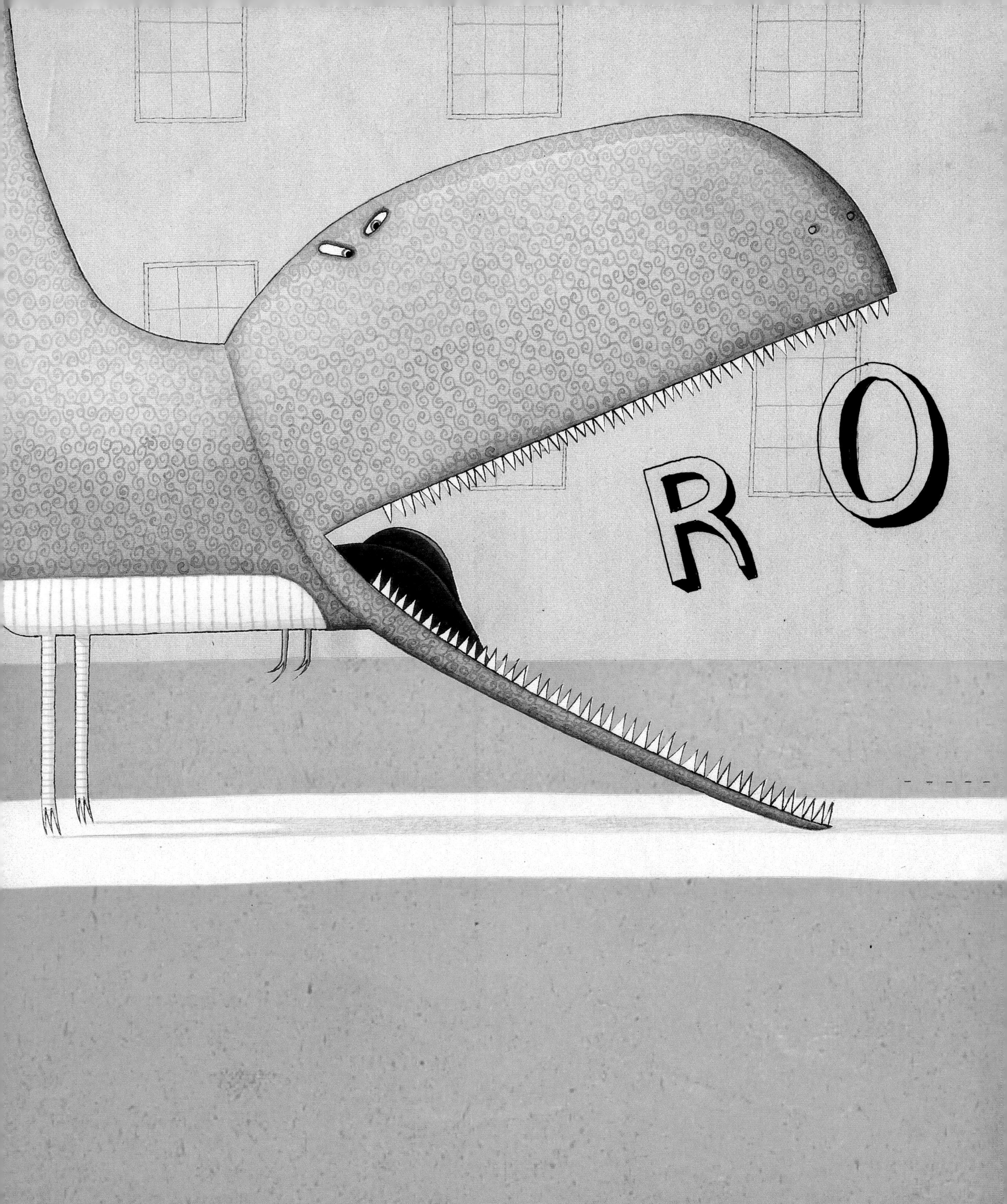
R O

AR!!

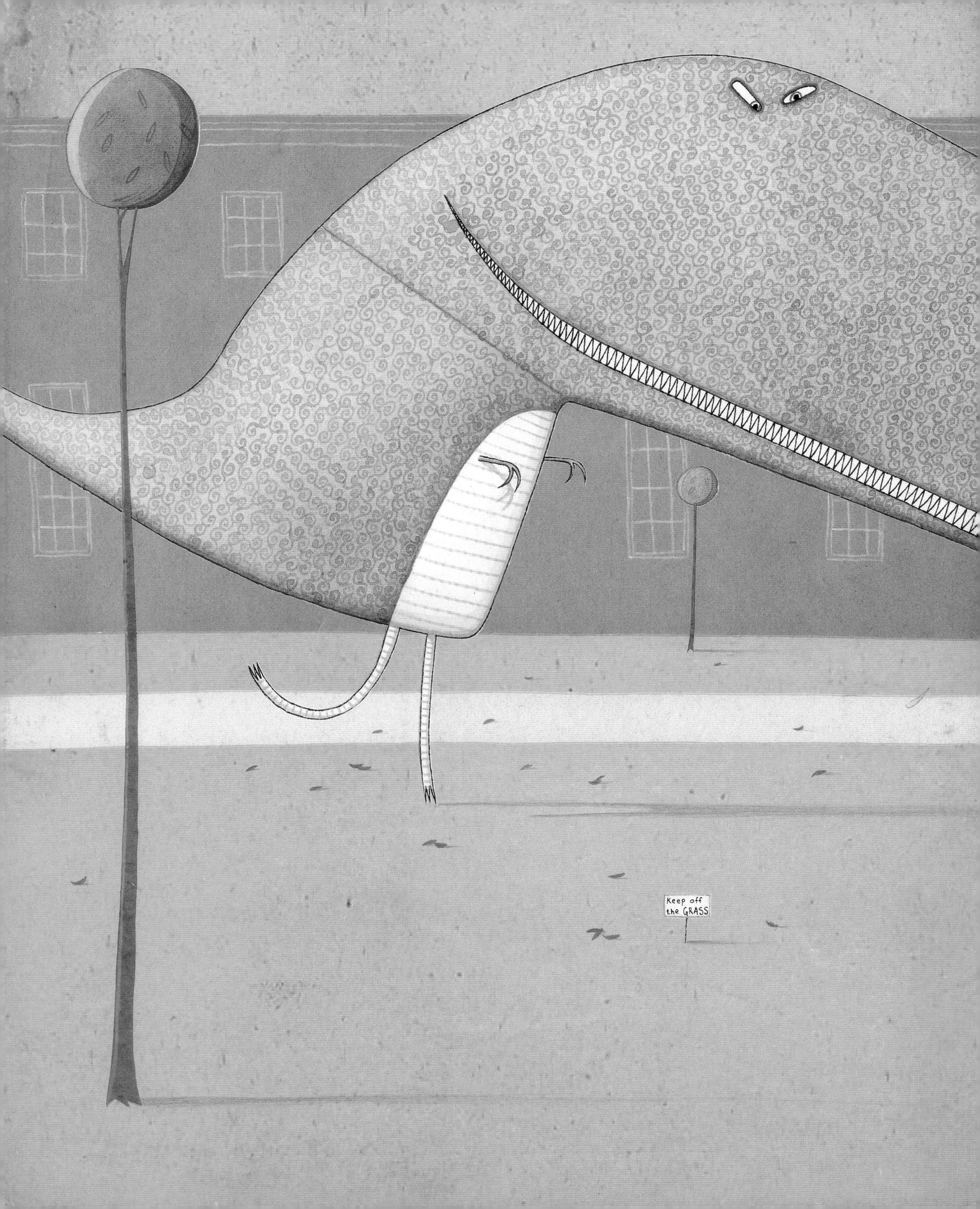
Keep off
the GRASS

"Oh! You're right, Dave," said Dad. "**That** dinosaur's not *dead*."

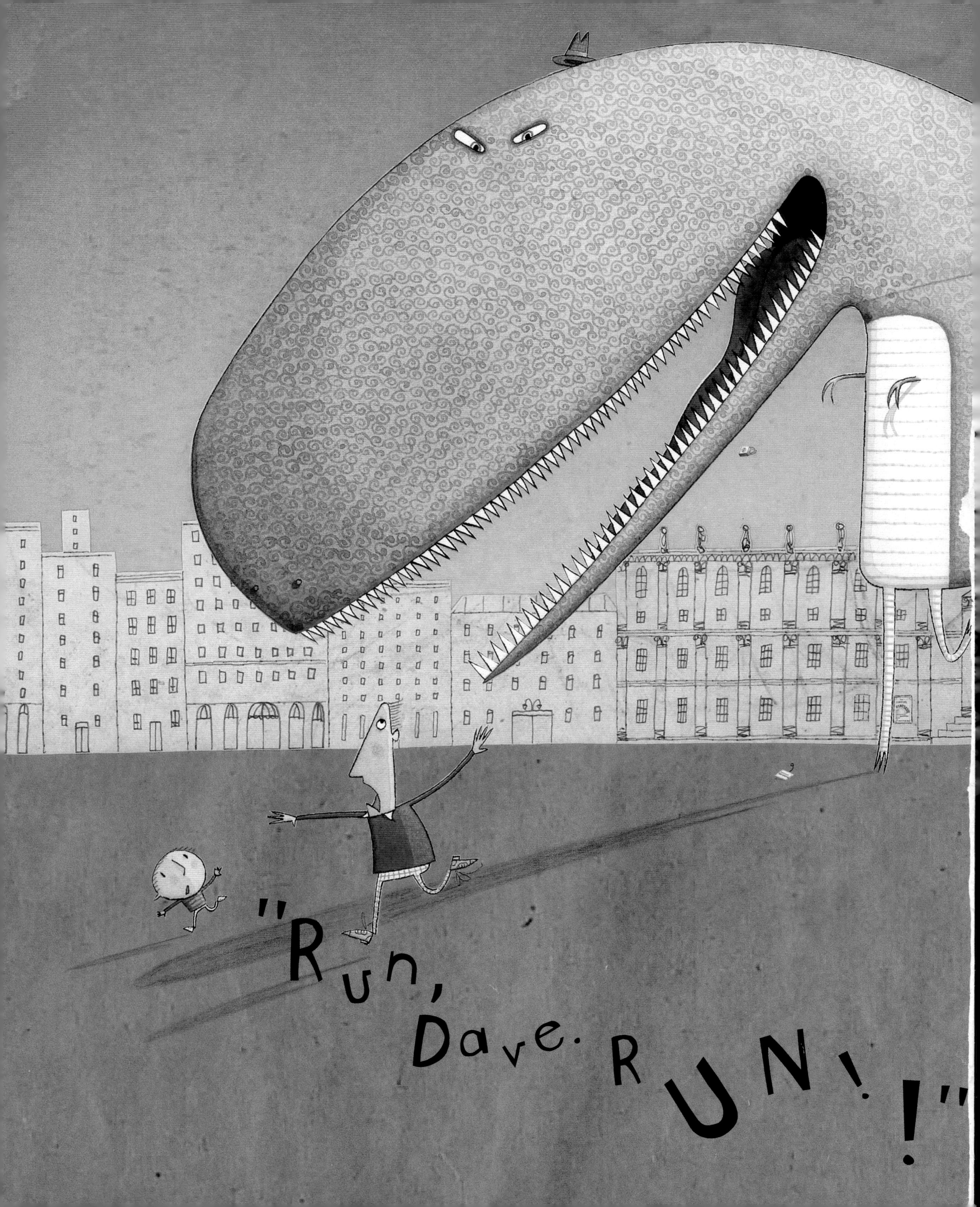
"Run, Dave. RUN!!"